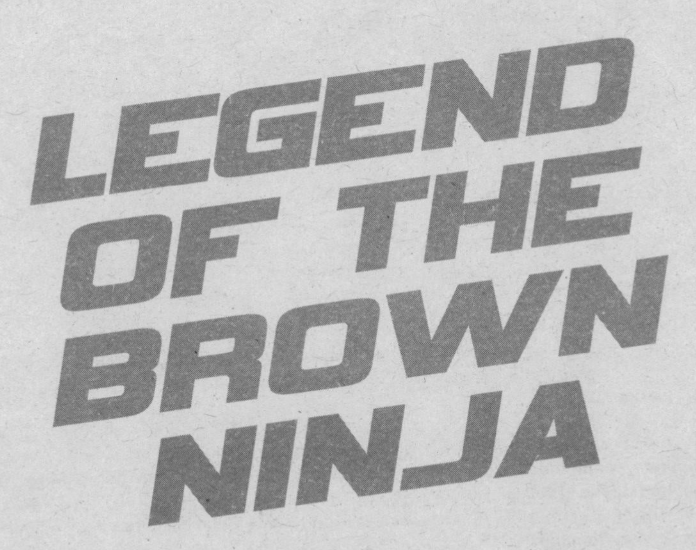

By Meredith Rusu

SCHOLASTIC INC.

Published by Scholastic Inc., *Publishers since 1920.* SCHOLASTIC and associated logos are trademarks and/or registered trademarks of Scholastic Inc.

ISBN 978-1-338-04466-9
10 9 8 7 6 5 4 3 2 17 18 19 20
Printed in the U.S.A. 40
First printing 2016

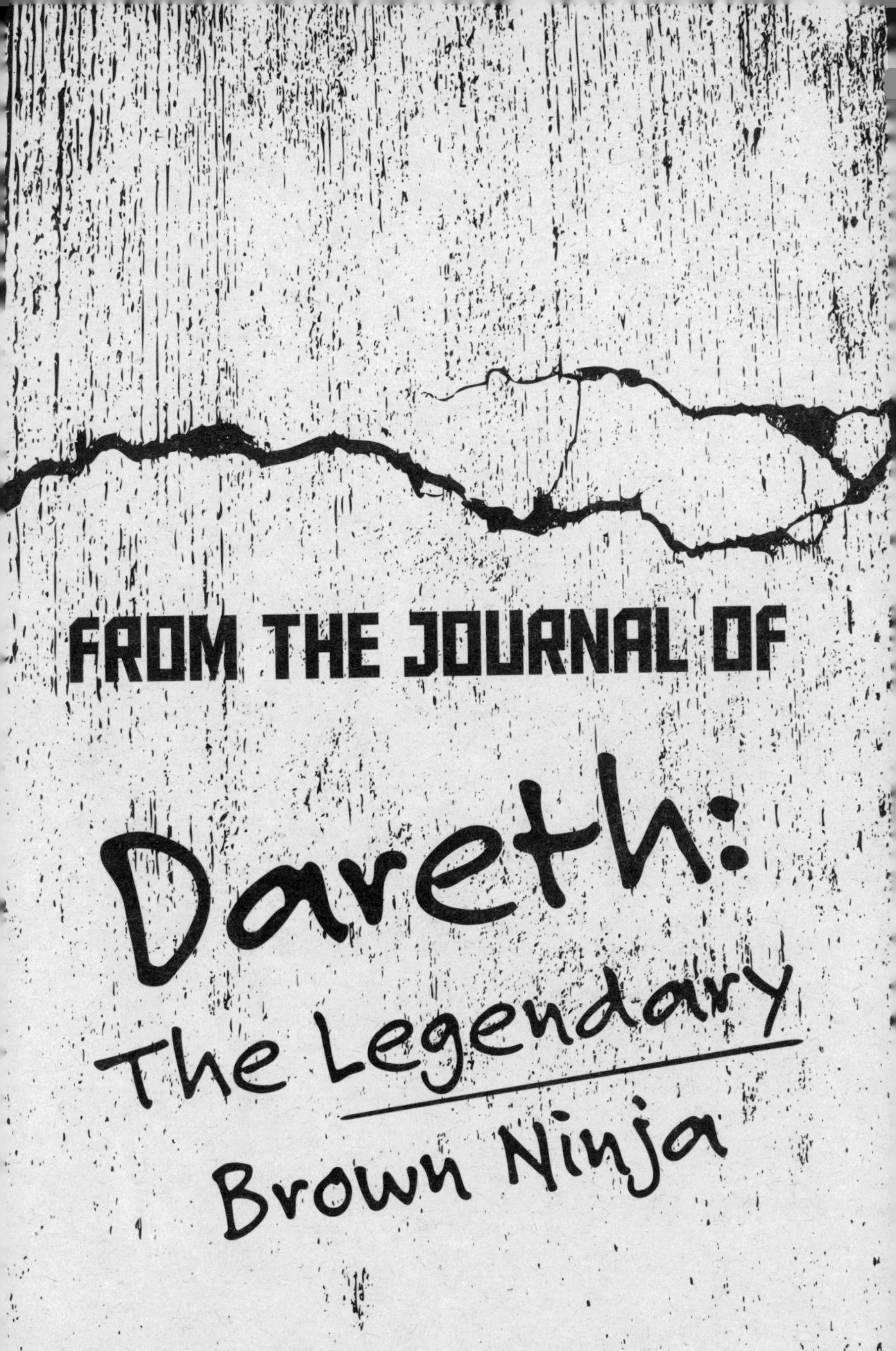
FROM THE JOURNAL OF
Dareth:
The Legendary
Brown Ninja

Dareth's Super-Secret, Ninja PR Journal
Entry #76
No one will ever find this, but if they do, it'll be worth a lot someday!

Trouble in Ninja Paradise

The ninja resist me.

You would think, since I'm their publicity manager, that the ninja would be thrilled to have me working for them. After all, I have their best interests at heart. All I want to do is make sure the world recognizes them for their total, incredible, amazing awesomeness!

But alas, things have turned bad. Sour. Nastier than two-day-old noodles. And I have no idea why.

I mean, sure, the ninja may have sent me a few texts. Left a voice mail or two. Something about "wanting to focus on being a team." But I assumed they were joking.

Who wants to focus on "being a team" when you can focus on being megastars!

Ugh. I better start at the beginning.

Since defeating the Preeminent, the ninja have been more popular than ever. People line up for blocks to catch just a glimpse of them in action! Clearly, they needed a manager.

That's where I came to the rescue. I, Dareth, the Legendary Brown Ninja, selflessly offered to be their guide to stardom. Their social media guru. The visionary that would take them from newbies to superstars.

For a while, things were going great. Promotional spots. Commercials. An unauthorized documentary. The fans were loving it, baby! They couldn't get enough!

But then, the unthinkable happened.

The ninja canceled a prime-time spot on Ninjago City's hottest talk show — Fred

Finley Live at Five. Canceled it! Don't they know how hard it is to get a guest spot on Fred Finley Live at Five? It's HARD.

I was sure they would be thrilled when I told them about the interview!

"Thank you, Dareth, for making us famous!" they would say.

"Thank you, Dareth, for brilliantly handling our public image!"

"Thank you, Dareth, for being the best thing that's ever happened to us!!"

Was that how it went down? No, it was not.

There's only so much one publicity manager can do. How am I supposed to keep the ninja up in the fan polls if they refuse to do public appearances?

This calls for drastic action. The ninja are my friends, and I can't let them down. Even if they don't realize it, there is nothing more fulfilling in life than being famous and popular.

Well, and maybe Master Chen's Puffy Potstickers. Those are very fulfilling.

So, okay. Popularity and potstickers. That's what life's all about.

I will make the ninja famous, or my name isn't Dareth!

(aka the Legendary Brown Ninja)

(aka PR Master/ Social Media Guru)

(Available for consultation and all your celebrity ninja needs)

Chapter 1

Looking good, Nya!"

Kai watched proudly as his sister took out three consecutive practice targets with one smooth water blast.

BLAM! BLAM! BLAM!

"You're on fire today!" Kai said. "And that's saying something coming from the master of *fi-yaaa*!"

He somersaulted next to her and blasted one of the dummies with a well-aimed fireball.

"Thanks," Nya said. "But I'm just getting started. In fact, I think I'm in need of a spark."

Nya looked at Jay and winked. Jay gave her a wide smile. Then he zapped a bolt of electricity right at her!

Without missing a beat, Nya blocked the electricity with a burst of water. It created an electrified arc that sprayed out at the remaining targets. *Zzzzzfttttt!* The dummies were obliterated.

"Time to clean up the mess," said an invisible voice above them.

In a *poof,* Cole appeared, hovering over the center of the training area. Since Cole was a ghost, he was able to vanish and reappear. He began whirling around faster and faster until he created an Airjitzu tornado powerful enough to lift all the broken dummy pieces off the deck of the *Destiny's Bounty.*

"Zane, Lloyd, you're up!" he called.

"Indeed," replied Zane. The Titanium Ninja powered up an ice blast while Lloyd generated a green energy ball. But instead of firing their elemental powers in one shot, the two ninja allowed their combined energy to drift into the whirling Airjitzu tornado.

Slowly, Lloyd's green energy began melding the debris together while Zane's ice surrounded it. In a bright burst of light, the tornado vanished. All that was left on the deck of the *Destiny's Bounty* was a smooth metal sphere constructed out of practice dummy remnants. It was icy to the touch.

"Well done, ninja," said Master Wu. He had been watching the practice session from his seat atop the *Destiny's Bounty* side rail. He was drinking tea, naturally.

"You're working very well as a team today," Wu noted. "Very in sync with one another."

"I must agree," said Zane. "Not to 'float our own boat,' but we are operating at maximum efficiency."

"It's like something's changed," said Lloyd, placing a hand on the cool sphere. "Like there's a different energy among all of us." He glanced over at Nya and Jay.

"Maybe that's because we feel like more of a team than ever before," said Jay. He took Nya's hand, and she smiled.

A lot *had* changed for the ninja. But only Jay and Nya knew the full truth.

Not long ago, the ninja had been attacked by a legendary wish-granting djinn named Nadakhan. For hundreds of years, Nadakhan had been trapped in the Teapot of Tyrahn. But an evil sorcerer named Clouse had released him. Once free, Nadakhan planned to build a sky world called Djinjago out of pieces stolen from New Ninjago City. He was obsessed with destroying the ninja and claiming Nya as his bride.

The only reason Nadakhan had been released from his lamp in the first place was because the ninja were wrapped up in one of Dareth's silly publicity stunts, and they weren't able to stop Clouse from summoning him.

Luckily, Jay had been able to undo all of Nadakhan's evil work with his final wish: that no one had ever found the teapot in the first place. Since Nadakhan was a djinn, he had to grant the wish. In doing so, time went back to the moment right before the Teapot of Tyrahn had been discovered.

No one remembered any of the events that had taken place, except for Jay and Nya. They had shared a lot during the adventure, and they'd grown close. Nya had once been uncertain if she liked Jay or not, but she was certain now. The bond they shared was very strong, and that made them both happy.

"I'm glad we decided to take a break from Dareth's publicity stunts for a while," Nya said. She carried a fresh training dummy out of a storage closet. "Being in the limelight was getting to be too much."

"And making us forget who we really are," Jay added.

"Speak for yourselves," Kai said. "I was enjoying the celebrity lifestyle."

"You do have the most Chirp followers," Zane pointed out.

"Speaking of Chirp," said Lloyd, "Kai, your phone is chirping."

Kai rushed to his phone. "Must be one of my adoring fans, looking to see why I've gone offline. My followers have needs, you know!"

Kai picked up his phone. His face fell.

"Aww, it's just Dareth," he said, putting the phone on speaker.

"Ninja, are you there?" Dareth's voice rang out. "Thank goodness I've reached you. Now, I know you said you weren't doing *Fred Finley Live at Five*, but I've just found out that . . . wait for it . . . they're making the entire show a *dedicated tribute* to your work. It's no longer just a guest spot — you'll be on the air for the entire hour!"

The ninja looked at one another.

"Sorry, Dareth," Lloyd spoke for all of them. "But we told you, we're taking a break from the celebrity life."

"To focus on ourselves," Cole added.

"As a team," Jay and Nya said together.

Kai frowned. Nya elbowed him.

"Yeah, yeah." Kai sighed. "Time off just to be ninja. The regular, old, 'we don't need action figures made of us' ninja."

"But . . . you don't understand . . ." Dareth sputtered. "The fans . . . the commitment . . . the PROMOTIONAL ENDORSEMENTS. You can't cancel!"

"You're right," said Nya. "*We* can't cancel, because *we* never booked it in the first place."

"Sorry, Dareth, but that's just not us anymore," said Lloyd. "We don't want to be famous."

There was a long pause on the other end of the line.

"But . . . that's just it!" exclaimed Dareth. "This talk show *isn't* about the ninja as celebrities. No! It's about you! Uh, as a team! Yeah — an entire hour dedicated to who you *really are.* All of New Ninjago City is inspired by you! We just want to give your fans the real story behind your teamwork."

Lloyd raised an eyebrow. "I don't know, Dareth. It still sounds like a publicity stunt."

"I swear it's not," insisted Dareth. "Hey, come on, ninja baby, you're talking to Dareth. I listened to you! 'No more publicity stunts, Dareth,' you said. Well, I can guarantee you that this is *not* a publicity stunt. This is the interview that will show everyone just what you stand for. Working together. Inspiring your fans to be their best! Nothing but total commitment. Reach for the . . ."

As Dareth nattered on, Lloyd put the phone on mute. "What do you guys think?" he asked.

Kai shrugged. "Could it really hurt? It would be nice to have a chance to explain to my — uh, our — fans why we're leaving the spotlight."

"I guess *one* more interview isn't so bad," said Jay.

"As long as we get to focus on who we are as a team," said Nya.

"Right," said Cole. "Something really inspiring."

Lloyd nodded. He turned the speaker-phone back on.

"Okay, Dareth," he said. "We'll do it. As long as you *promise* this interview will focus on us as a team."

The ninja could practically hear Dareth jumping for joy on the other end of the line.

"You got it, ninja! I promise, this will be the interview to end all interviews. Or my name isn't Dareth the Brown Ninja!"

Chapter 2

A few days later, the ninja were seated comfortably on a long couch next to Fred Finley. They watched the camera lights blinking, signaling the show was about to start.

"All right, ninja, we're about to *ninja-go*!" Fred Finley flashed an impossibly white smile. "You guys all set?"

"Yeah." Lloyd nodded. "We're ready."

Cole leaned forward so he could see Fred Finley from the end of the couch. "Just to make sure, Dareth told you what we want to focus this interview on, right? It's about our work as a team."

Fred Finley's smile grew wider. "Oh, he sure did. Trust me, this is going to be the interview that really lifts the mask off the ninja!"

The ninja glanced at one another as the camera lights blinked more rapidly. From the wings, Dareth gave them a big thumbs-up.

"And three, two, one," a cameraman announced. "We're live!"

"Welcome!" said Fred Finley. "To another exciting episode of . . ."

"*FRED FINLEY LIVE AT FIVE*!" cheered the studio audience. "Live at Five! Live at Five!"

Fred Finley did a little dance for the audience as they clapped and chanted.

"All right, folks," said Fred. "Today, I have six very special guests with me. You guessed it . . . the heroes you've all been dying to get the *real* story behind . . . Ninjago City's very own NINJA!"

The audience went wild. Kai waved to the fans, brushed his hair back, and pointed to two girls in the audience. They swooned.

Meanwhile, Jay and Nya fidgeted. This wasn't starting off like a serious interview.

"So, ninja." Fred turned his attention to them. "Let's get right to business. Tell us — what's going on?"

"Uh, well," said Lloyd. "I'm glad you asked. We're working together as a team. Stronger than ever."

"That's right," said Jay. "We're very in sync."

"In fact," said Nya, "you may have heard that we're taking a break from celebrity life."

The audience *oooooohhhed.*

"Oh, yes, we have heard that." Fred Finley glanced at Jay, and then at Nya. "But tell us, is that the *whole* story?"

Jay and Nya looked at each other, unsettled.

"Um, yeah," said Nya. "What do you mean?"

"I mean . . ." Fred Finley leaned closer. "Are you sure there isn't more to it?"

Zane jumped in. "Quite sure. If you'll excuse me, Fred, I am confused. Your question implies there is unsavory information we are not sharing. But that is not the point of this interview."

"Yeah," Cole said. "This is supposed to be about our work as a team."

"You know, for our fans to see what we're all about," said Kai.

Fred Finley leaned back. "Oh, it is!" he said. "Folks, it looks like the ninja may need a little help telling the real story. Shall we go to the *Real Reel*?"

"Yeah!" cheered the crowd. "Run that reel!"

The ninja watched, stunned, as an oversized movie screen lowered behind them. A moment later, it lit up with the name of the segment in big, bold letters:

Trouble in Ninja Paradise!

"Trouble? What trouble?!" exclaimed Jay.

Secret-camera-style footage of the ninja splashed across the big screen. It showed them walking through town, eating noodles at Master Chen's, even attending publicity events. But the way the footage was all pieced together, it made it look like there was, well, *drama*!

"Nya, Nya!" On the screen, a cameraman jostled Nya on the street. "Jay or Cole?"

"Seriously?" onscreen Nya answered, pushing the camera away. "Not a chance!"

On the couch, Nya flushed. That had been before she and Jay had grown closer. She hadn't realized how harsh she'd sounded back then.

The footage cut to a shot of Jay talking with reporters outside a florist shop. He was carrying a beautiful bouquet of flowers.

"These are for that one special lady in my life . . ." Jay told the reporters.

"Ooooooooooh," the studio audience echoed.

"Wait!" Jay cried. "It was Mother's Day. Those flowers were for my mother!"

But the film cut away before Jay got to that part of his interview. Instead, it jumped to a shot of Kai.

"Of course I'm the best-looking," Kai told a reporter. "My hair is on *fi-yaa*!"

"Aw, come on," Kai complained from the couch. "I had just gotten a haircut!"

The film reel cut to a shot of Cole, Lloyd, and Zane. They were laughing.

"He's got the power of hot air," Lloyd told the reporters. "He's not really a ninja."

The audience gasped.

"We were talking about Dareth, not Kai!" Lloyd insisted. "That reporter asked us what power the Brown Ninja had."

"I think we've seen enough," said Nya. With a quick motion, she fired a ball of water right at the screen. It crashed to the ground in a damp heap.

"Awwwwww," said the audience.

But Fred Finley was still smiling. "A little *too* much reality?" he asked. "Then tell us, ninja. What is the real story?"

"The real story is that this interview is done," said Lloyd. He and the other ninja stood up. "We're a team," Lloyd continued. "We're at our best when we're together. And anyone who says otherwise is just looking for publicity."

Lloyd shot Dareth a look. Dareth gulped.

The audience groaned as the ninja walked off the set.

"Well, folks, it looks like our guests got a little too close to the truth for comfort," said Fred Finley. "But that's okay, because we've got the rest of the story . . . on our backup *Real Reel*!"

"YAY!" the audience cried as an even bigger movie screen lowered from the ceiling.

Backstage, the ninja confronted Dareth.

"What *was* that?" Cole demanded.

"I . . . I have no idea where that came from," Dareth said. "Fred told me the interview would get to the core of who you guys really are."

"By humiliating us?" asked Kai. "Where did he even get the idea for *Trouble in Ninja Paradise*?"

"Ah, well." Dareth pulled at his shirt collar. "I may have mentioned it was a catchy title . . ."

"You promised us this interview would inspire our fans because it was all about teamwork. It wasn't supposed to pit us against one another!" said Lloyd.

"Well, it was getting to that," Dareth insisted. "You didn't give Fred a chance . . ."

"No, we gave *you* a chance," said Zane. "And we were wrong."

"That's it, Dareth," said Nya. "No more publicity. No more bookings. We're done."

"But . . . but . . ." Dareth pleaded.

"Don't call us again unless Ninjago City is in trouble," said Lloyd. "Because that's the only thing we're doing now. Working together to keep people safe. Come on, guys."

Dareth was speechless. How could the ninja walk away from so much potential?

Didn't they realize how hard he had worked to make them famous? And wasn't being famous the most important thing there was?

Something had to be done.

"Unavailable unless Ninjago City is in trouble," Dareth mumbled to himself.

A sneaky glint came to his eye.

"Well, then, we'll just see what we can do about that."

Chapter 3

A few weeks later, the ninja were eating at one of their favorite restaurants. But their definition of "favorite" had changed since they'd become famous.

Their old favorite restaurant was Master Chen's Noodle House. But once fans realized that Master Chen's was their favorite hangout, their admirers started stalking the ninja there. So they had to switch to Master Soba's Soup Shop.

Then, after the *Live at Five* blowup, the paparazzi had started harassing the ninja

like never before. Apparently, the only thing more intriguing to fans than a group of masked heroes was a group of masked heroes with *drama*.

So now the ninja were forced to go to Biker Barry's Buffalo Wings Bar. It was the only place in town with food so lousy, there were no regulars. Even still, the ninja had taken to wearing hats and glasses to avoid being spotted.

"Man, what I wouldn't give for some puffy potstickers." Cole sighed as he tossed a hot wing back into the basket. "Not gonna lie, Biker Barry needs to work on his recipe."

"This is all Dareth's fault," Nya complained. "If it weren't for him, we could still be going for noodles like normal."

"At least he hasn't been bothering us," Lloyd pointed out. "Have any of you heard from him since the talk show?"

Cole, Jay, Kai, Nya, and Zane all shook their heads. It did indeed seem like Dareth had dropped off the face of Ninjago City. Not one voice mail, text — not even a Chirp.

"Maybe he really didn't realize things were going to go that way on Fred Finley's show," said Kai. "Maybe it was all a big misunderstanding."

Cole, Jay, Lloyd, Nya, and Zane shot Kai a look.

Kai sighed. "Yeah. You're probably right."

"On the bright side," said Zane, "social science does indicate that without the continued stimuli, the public will, in time, lose interest in our status."

"In English, Zane?" asked Jay.

"He means 'out of sight, out of mind,'" said Cole. "And Zane's right. As long as there's no big bad attacking Ninjago City, we just need to sit back, relax, and wait for this all to blow over —"

Kai's phone suddenly started buzzing.

"You have GOT to be kidding me," said Kai. "It's Dareth."

Nya grabbed Kai's phone. "Whatever you want, Dareth, we're not interested."

"Ninja! Nin . . . iz . . . that . . . you?" Dareth's voice came through the speaker. But it sounded garbled.

"Of course it is," said Nya. "*You* called us."

"Trouble . . . need help . . . downtowzzzzzz . . . Dr . . ."

Dareth's voice buzzed out.

"Did he say trouble?" asked Lloyd.

"Yeah, downtown," said Kai.

"Do you think it's a trick?" asked Cole.

The ninja looked at one another, uncertain.

"I guess there's only one way to find out," said Lloyd. "*Ninja-GO!*"

The ninja whirled downtown in a flurry of Airjitzu. What they saw when they arrived made their jaws drop.

"I don't believe it," said Zane.

"It's not possible," breathed Kai.

Circling Cyrus Borg Industries, with moonlight glinting off their shiny scales, were . . .

"Dragons!" exclaimed Nya. "But — how?"

"Oh, thank GOODNESS!" a voice cried out behind them. Dareth raced up to the ninja. "I wasn't sure if you would come. But you're here! And we're saved!"

"What's going on, Dareth?" asked Lloyd. "How are there dragons downtown?"

"I don't know!" cried Dareth. "One minute, everything is peaceful, and then BAM! Dragons! You're the only ones who can stop them, ninja."

Cole looked up. There were one, two, three. Three dragons. Each a different color and crying out in high-pitched screeches.

"Maybe they're friendly?" Cole suggested tentatively.

BOOM!

One of the dragons smashed its tail into

the side of Borg Industries. It shattered a part of the building!

"I'm guessing not," said Kai.

"What do we do?" asked Jay.

"First we stop them from destroying downtown," said Lloyd. "Then we figure out where they came from."

"Right," the ninja agreed. They each powered up their own Elemental Dragons and rose into the sky.

"Ninja-GO!"

Nya swooped up toward one of the dragons. It looked like a fiery red serpent with clawed wings and a long, whiskered snout. It screeched at her angrily.

"How about you just chill out," Nya shouted at the dragon. With an effort, she powered up a huge water ball.

The dragon opened its gaping jaws and *FWOOM!* It shot out a blazing streak of flame directly at Nya. She dodged out of the way just in time.

"Holy smokes! They can breathe fire?" Nya exclaimed.

"Looks like it," shouted Kai. "But if I've learned anything, it's that the only way to fight fire is with fire!"

Kai shot a whirling ball of flame toward the blue dragon in the center of the trio. It looked like it would be a direct hit, until:

Fzzzzt!

The fireball hit an invisible shield surrounding the dragon and was extinguished.

Kai's jaw dropped. "Uh, okay, I've heard of dragons breathing fire. But dragons with shields?"

"This is like something out of one of Fritz Donegon's sci-fi movies!" Jay exclaimed. "And *not* in a good way!"

The ninja watched dumbfounded as the dragons continued to circle Borg Industries.

"Why aren't they leaving the tower?" Nya asked. "What do they want?"

"An interesting observation," said Zane

thoughtfully. "Pixal, please scan the source of the dragons' shields."

"Scanning . . ." Pixal replied. "Data incomplete. I need to be closer to generate a full bioscan."

Zane nodded. "Understood." He shot up toward the dragons.

"Zane, be careful!" cried Lloyd. "And watch out for the —"

But before Lloyd could finish, the third yellow dragon dipped out of formation. It snaked around the building and came up . . . right behind Zane!

"LOOK OUT!" cried Lloyd.

But it was too late. The dragon unleashed an enormous burst of yellow-green flame, engulfing the Titanium Ninja!

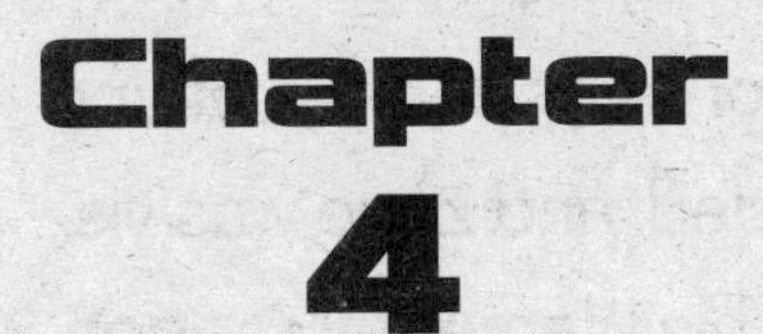

Chapter 4

ZANE!" cried the ninja.

Zane's friends watched in shock as the unearthly flames surrounded their friend, blocking him from view.

"Nya, quick!" yelled Jay. "You're the only one who can stop it!"

Snapping out of it, Nya summoned all the water strength she had. With a gigantic wave, she sent a wall of water hurling toward the flames. The water impacted! And then . . .

. . . it continued straight through the fire, arcing back down toward the ground as if it hadn't hit anything at all. It didn't even evaporate.

The ninja stared, completely confused.

"What's happening?" Nya asked.

Suddenly, the dragon stopped breathing its fire. The blaze subsided, and Zane was visible again, hovering on his Elemental Dragon.

"Zane! Are you okay?" cried Cole.

The Nindroid looked down at himself. He was completely unharmed.

"I am," Zane said, equally stunned. He looked up at the yellow dragon as it returned to formation. "A hologram?" he asked.

"Cut, cut, cut!" cried Dareth from somewhere below.

The ninja looked down to see Dareth wheeling up with a camera crew behind him.

"Dareth!" shouted Kai. "What is going on?"

"I'll tell you what's going on," exclaimed Dareth. "I'm restoring your image as the heroes of Ninjago!"

The six ninja flew down to the ground and

dematerialized their Elemental Dragons. Up above, Dareth's "dragons" resumed circling Borg Industries.

"They are holograms," Zane announced. "Digital representations giving the illusion of —"

"The actual thing!" exclaimed Cyrus Borg. He wheeled up excitedly toward the group. "So good to see you all again, ninja. I trust you're well. Very exciting, isn't it? Holographic creatures real enough to pass as the actual things. This will revolutionize the film industry!"

"But we saw one of the dragons hit the building," insisted Nya. "It caused damage."

Cyrus Borg nodded happily. "Computerized frequencies set to cause predetermined sections of the building to fall off. Look — my Repair-o-bots are fixing the building as we speak!"

Everyone looked upward to see dozens of tiny robots with multiple legs and long

claw arms replacing the broken pieces of the building.

"Ingenious, no?" Cyrus smiled. "Think of what this means. Entire action sequences — like the one you six were kind enough to just run through — will be entirely possible without digital editing. Incredible!"

Lloyd shook his head. "Sorry to disappoint you, Cyrus. But we didn't know this was a trial run. In fact, we didn't know this was staged at all."

Cyrus seemed genuinely confused. "But Dareth said you were all excited to test out my new holographic dragon program?"

Everyone turned to look at Dareth.

"Ah, well," Dareth stammered. He cast a furtive glance at the film crew behind him. "Quick! Take the footage to the editing room and get it prepped!"

"Dareth!" yelled Cole. "This is not cool!"

"I know, I know," whined Dareth. "But you guys left me no choice. After the *Fred Finley* fiasco, *someone* had to restore your public image. I knew the only way to get you back in the game was with some action! And boy, was that some action! All that *Live at Five* drama will be old news when your fans see this. Ninja versus dragons? It's perfect! I'm thinking a viral web movie. A fan poll voting which one of you should face off against what creature next. We're heading back to the top, baby!"

"If you pull a stunt like this again, you just might find yourself heading to the hospital," Nya muttered.

Dareth arched an eyebrow. "To the hospital . . . because you'll be doing a promotional meet-and-greet with the patients?" he asked hopefully.

"NO!" the ninja yelled back.

"Don't call us again unless there are REAL bad guys to fight," said Lloyd.

"In fact, don't call us at all," added Jay. "Consider your number permanently blocked."

Chapter 5

Later, Dareth sat at Master Chen's Noodle House, sulking over a glass of ginger ale.

"'Don't call us at all,'" he mimicked Jay's voice. "'Consider yourself permanently blocked.'"

"Something got you down, friend?" The hostess walked up behind the counter. It was Skylor.

Skylor was a friend of the ninja. In fact, she was an Elemental Master with the power of Amber. That meant she could absorb other fighters' strengths and use them as her own. These days, however, she'd retired from fighting to run her father's old noodle shop. The only "absorbing" she did was listening to customers' stories. But she enjoyed the company, and people appreciated her advice.

"I've seen that look before," she told Dareth. "Having an argument with a friend?"

Dareth scoffed. "Six of them. And they'd be the biggest names in Ninjago, too, if they'd just listen to my advice!"

Skylor looked more closely at Dareth. "Say, I know you. I remember seeing you with the ninja. What's your name again? Darren?"

Dareth puffed out his chest. "Dareth. Legendary Brown Ninja and Public Relations Guru." He sighed. "At least, I was."

"Yeah, I remember now," Skylor said. "You're the one in the background of all the ninjas' television interviews, running around and giving orders." Skylor chuckled. "Well, if you're arguing with the ninja, I can tell you this much. They're stubborn. It's going to be

hard to get them to do something they don't want to do."

Dareth shook his head forlornly. "Tell me about it. I can't believe this is happening. All that time spent scheduling interviews. Begging for corporate sponsors. Chasing down producers as they left their offices. All for nothing. Everything is just slipping away."

As Dareth spoke, there was a small commotion by the noodle bar's television.

"Hey, you mind turning it up?" A patron across the restaurant pointed to the TV.

Skylor raised the volume, and everyone watched as a breaking news alert flashed across the screen.

"This just in," the announcer said. "*Another* inmate has broken out of Kryptorium Prison and made it all the way to the streets of Ninjago City."

The program showed security camera footage of an escaped prisoner sneaking down an alley. It was Wyplash — one of the skeleton warriors the ninja had captured and sent to jail long ago.

"Luckily," the announcer said, "security footage from Cyrus Borg's new Street-Safe Technology led to the convict's recapture by Ninjago Police. But the question remains, how are so many inmates breaking out of jail?"

The footage switched to a shot of police officers cornering the surprised Wyplash and handcuffing him. In the background was Warden Noble, the head guard at Kryptorium Prison.

"We're launching a full investigation," Warden Noble promised. "We won't rest until we figure out how and why this is happening."

Skylor shook her head. "If I were you, that's the 'slipping away' I'd be worried about. Not interviews or sponsors. Kryptorium Prison holds some real baddies, and most of them are in there thanks to the ninja. I'm sure a lot of those thugs would just love to sneak out and settle a score or two."

Skylor waited for Dareth to respond. But he had grown quiet, lost in thought.

"*Real* baddies," he said slowly. "Settle a score. Of course! That's brilliant. I wish I'd thought of it myself. Oh, wait, I did!"

"Thought of what?" Skylor asked.

"No time to explain." Dareth jumped off his bar stool. "The Brown Ninja has work to do!"

Skylor watched Dareth race out through the restaurant's double doors. Then she shook her head. She knew the ninjas' powers pretty well. But she had a feeling the Brown Ninja's "powers" were in a league of their own.

Chapter 6

"Are you sure about this?" Jay looked down uneasily from his Elemental Dragon. Below, the Sea of Sand stretched for miles. And ahead on the horizon, Kryptorium Prison loomed.

"Yes," replied Lloyd. "The message was definitely from the warden. He said he needed help, and that's what we're going to do."

"What exactly did the warden say again?" Jay asked.

"He needs us to figure out how the prisoners have been escaping from their cells," said Zane. "Since we have prior experience breaking out inmates, the warden thought we would be the perfect candidates to solve the mystery."

"Oh, yeah, I guess we do have that expertise," Kai said. He sighed, reminiscing. "Breaking out Pythor. Stopping Chen's legion of fake Anacondrai. Ah, those were the good old days."

"Speak for yourself," said Jay. "I, for one, never wanted to see Kryptorium Prison again. Being locked up there once was enough for me."

Lloyd looked at Jay, confused. "What are you talking about? When were you locked up in Kryptorium?"

"Oh, uh," Jay stammered. "It's a figure of speech. I meant, I've seen enough of it to last me a lifetime. Heh, heh."

Jay and Nya shared a look. Sometimes they forgot the other ninja didn't remember their adventure against Nadakhan. The truth was, all six of them had been imprisoned in the Kryptorium for a while as they were battling the djinn. But only Jay and Nya remembered that.

"Well, we won't stay long," said Lloyd. "We'll see what we can do to help Warden Noble and then head back."

The ninja swooped down toward the entrance of the Kryptorium. It was eerily quiet.

"I thought the warden was going to meet us at the front door?" Nya said.

"Me, too," said Lloyd. "Something's fishy. Keep your guard up."

Cole, Jay, Kai, Lloyd, Nya, and Zane carefully made their way into the massive building. One by one, the metal doors leading deeper into the prison opened for them.

As they passed through the last set of doors, they reached a wide, darkened hallway.

"This is really creeping me out . . ." said Jay.

"Warden Noble?" Lloyd called. "Are you here? It's us — the ninja."

"The niiiiiiinjaaaaaaa."

Voices suddenly echoed from the walls around them.

Instantly, the previous set of metal doors they'd just stepped through slammed shut.

Jay raced up to them and pounded. "We're locked in!" he cried.

The lights suddenly snapped on brighter. Sinister laughter filled the hallway.

The ninja turned to see all of Kryptorium's inmates staring out at them from their cells.

They were locked in with the prisoners!

Up in the warden's office, Dareth and Warden Noble watched the action on surveillance camera screens.

"Now, you're sure the ninja will be able to figure out how the prisoners keep secretly escaping?" Warden Noble asked, taking a sip of his coffee.

Dareth slurped an iced frappé through a straw. "Of course, Warden. You can count on my ninja to solve the problem."

The warden watched the screen closely. "Tell me again why we can't be there while the ninja are talking to the prisoners? Seems a bit dramatic for my taste."

Dareth grinned. "Trust me. My ninja are at their best when they're in action." He produced a movie camera. "And we're going to catch it all on tape!"

Down below, the ninja looked around nervously as the inmates heckled them from behind bars.

"Well, I'll be charmed. Who do we have here?" said Captain Soto. "It be the pajama men, come to visit us."

"Guys, now I'm really freaking out!" said Jay.

It was hard not to be intimidated. All the ninjas' old foes were there. Captain Soto and his pirate crew. The skeleton warriors, Nuckal, Kruncha, and Wyplash. There were even a Stone Warrior and a few Nindroids left over from the Digital Overlord days.

Lloyd frowned, unfazed. "Where's the warden?" he demanded. "What have you done with him?"

The inmates just laughed.

One of them stepped up to the bars from the shadows of his cell. The ninja had never seen this guy before. He had a robotic arm and a nasty scowl on his face.

"They call me the Mechanic," he rasped. "And I got a bone to pick with you."

Lloyd pointed to his robotic arm. "That's one more bone than you've got in your entire arm. Let me guess, you don't have much of a spine, either."

The ninja gasped. Those were fighting words!

"Lloyd, what are you doing?" hissed Cole.

"Acting tough," said Lloyd. "These guys only respond to one thing — tough."

The Mechanic growled. "I used to repair noodle trucks for Master Chen and his underground organization. When you put him out of business . . ."

"Yeah, yeah, we put you out of business, too," said Nya. She and Jay had actually heard all of this before, when they were locked up in the Kryptorium prison in the alternate timeline. "Guys, I think that's enough chitchat."

"Now tell us what you've done with the warden," said Kai. "Or do we have to knock it out of you?"

That just made the prisoners laugh harder.

"You hear that, boys?" said the Mechanic. "Sounds like the ninja want to roughhouse a bit. Normally I keep to myself. But this time, I feel like playing along."

The Mechanic suddenly produced a makeshift remote control. He pressed a button on it.

Whhhhhiiiirrrrrr.

All of the inmates' cell doors began rattling open!

"Uh, guys," Jay said nervously.

The prisoners cackled as they stepped free from their cells and circled the ninja.

"Fellas," said the Mechanic. "I think it's time we gave our guests a proper welcome."

Chapter 7

"Attack!" Captain Soto cried.

The inmates had the ninja completely surrounded. As one, they charged!

Lloyd somersaulted over two rushing prisoners and shot a blast of green energy at the center of the room. It acted like a mini earthquake, knocking any prisoners nearby off-balance.

Suddenly, something hard hit Lloyd's head.

"Ow!" he yelped, rubbing the back of his head. He looked around to find a skeleton arm lying nearby.

Kruncha laughed from across the room. "Told you we had a bone to pick with you!"

"Yeah, told you!" chuckled Nuckal. Then he looked down at his arm, which was missing. "Hey, wait," he said. "That was *my* bone!"

Meanwhile, Nya grabbed hold of Kai and swung him around feetfirst, knocking three Nindroids right back into their cells.

Clang, clang, clang!

"I think it's time for a reboot," Kai shouted. With a fire blast, he slammed the cell doors shut, melting the gates to the wall.

Across the room, Cole and Jay faced off against Soto's pirate crew.

"Pajama men!" said Soto. "Prepare to walk the plank."

"Oh, yeah?" said Jay. "Come and make me!"

"Arrrrrr!" The pirates rushed at Jay.

Jay waited until the last possible second . . . then he leaped out of the way in a whirlwind of Airjitzu! Behind him, Cole was ready. He used his Earth power to lift three stones up from the prison floor. Then he rolled them straight at Soto and his crew like bowling balls. The stones knocked them over one, two, three!

Jay landed beside the dazed pirates. "Didn't we ever tell you, guys?" he asked. "Pajama men don't sleep with the fishes!"

Then Jay noticed one of Soto's pirates had accidentally dropped his eye patch. "Cool!" he said, picking it up. "I kind of missed wearing one of these!"

Cole laughed. "I think it's time we put the rest of these guys on ice. Zane! What do you say we turn this place into a skating rink and send everyone flying back into their cells?"

But Zane didn't reply.

Cole looked around. "Zane?" he called.

While the other ninja were busy fighting, the Mechanic had cornered Zane in his cell.

"That's a lot of spare parts you got there, Nindroid," the Mechanic rasped. "I could use a few in a place like this."

"I am afraid they are not available," Zane replied. He tried to power up an ice blast. But to his surprise, his elemental power just fizzled out.

"Pixal, what is happening?" he asked.

"Scanning the cell. Stand by," said Pixal. A few seconds later, she gasped. "Zane, the insides of these bars are coated with vengestone. Your powers won't work in here."

The Mechanic laughed. "That's right. I've been tinkering with a trick or two in case you guys ever came to visit. Looks like it paid off. Let's get 'em, boys."

The Mechanic and his cronies piled on top of Zane. Without his ice power, Zane was helpless!

The Mechanic pulled open Zane's chest plate. "Well, I'll be. Look at all those spare parts."

"Brace yourself, Zane," said Pixal. "I am rerouting all remaining power to your chest. In three, two, one . . ."

ZAP! The jolt of energy blasted the Mechanic and his thugs right out of the cell!

"Thank you, Pixal!" exclaimed Zane.

"Nobody messes with my Nindroid," Pixal replied.

As Zane sat up, his friends all rushed into the cell to check on him.

"Zane! Are you okay?" Lloyd asked.

"Stop!" cried Zane. "This cell — it is a trap."

But it was too late. With a mechanical *clang*, the cell door rattled shut.

The inmates laughed as the ninja raced up to the bars. Kai tried to melt them, but his fire power barely created a spark.

"What's happening?" he asked.

Lloyd tried to create a ball of green energy, but to no avail. "Our powers. They're . . . gone?" he said.

"The bars are coated with vengestone," said Zane. "The Mechanic tricked us."

"You mean the Mechanic actually coated his prison bars on the *chance* we might come here one day?!" cried Jay. "This has got to be the worst luck ever!"

Across the prison hall, the Mechanic rose to his feet. He was visibly shaken by Zane's energy blast. But he was smiling. He waggled the remote control that operated the cell doors at the ninja.

"Looks like we're the ones in control now," he said.

Chapter 8

The ninja looked at one another. This was *not* good.

"What do we do?" asked Jay. "How do we get out without our powers?"

Lloyd angrily took hold of the cell bars. "This was a trap all along, wasn't it? You had the warden call us just to lure us in for a fight."

Soto shook his head. "Silly pajama men. It be *you* that came to *us*!"

"We didn't tell the warden nothin'," an inmate named Dan barked. "You came here all on your own."

"Then where is the warden?" demanded Cole. "What did you do to him?"

At that, all of the inmates shared a brief look of confusion.

"Uh, when is the last time we saw the warden?" asked Nuckal.

Kruncha bonked him on the head. "Who cares? He ain't here now."

The Mechanic glowered. "And it looks like he certainly doesn't care about you ninja."

"So you're telling us that the warden called us for help, and then just *happened* to disappear without a trace when we got here?" Cole asked. "And you don't think that's a little weird? Come on. We may have fallen into your trap, but we're not falling for that."

Little did the ninja know, things were about to get *so* much weirder.

"And . . . that's a wrap!"

A familiar voice suddenly echoed down the hall.

"Oh, no. This isn't happening," said Kai.

Walking toward them, movie camera in hand, was none other than Dareth. Behind him was the warden.

"DARETH!" the ninja all shouted at once.

"Ninja! My brave little ninja!" Dareth cried gleefully. "That. Was. Epic. Perfection! It couldn't have been better if I'd staged it myself. Oh, wait, I did!"

"Can someone please explain what's going on?" yelled Jay.

"Yes," chimed in Soto. "I, too, be confused."

"Well, you see" — Warden Noble adjusted his glasses — "Dareth came to me with an idea. He wanted me to ask you ninja to figure out how the inmates have been escaping."

The warden walked up to the Mechanic and pointed to the makeshift remote control that had opened the cell doors.

"Thanks to you ninja," the warden continued, "we have our culprit."

"Wait, I don't understand," said Nya. "The Mechanic has been letting prisoners go one by one? But why? Why didn't he just escape by himself?"

The Mechanic scowled. "Needed time to rebuild my business after you six destroyed it," he said. "And these inmates were each willing to give anything for a taste of freedom."

"So . . ." Lloyd said slowly. "This was all . . . a stunt? The fight wasn't real?"

"Oh, it was real!" exclaimed Dareth. "Real action! Real baddies! Just like you asked for! 'Don't call us, Dareth, unless there are real bad guys to fight.' And it was awesome. We got it all on tape! Wait until Ninjago City gets a load of the ninja fighting off an entire prison full of the baddest of the bad!"

"We could have gotten hurt, Dareth!" yelled Cole. "Sprocket-arm there nearly disassembled Zane."

"I must agree," said Zane. "This endeavor was not at all safe. I'm surprised, Warden, that you went along with it."

The warden coughed. "Well, we didn't know how the prisoners were escaping, so I had no idea they would all be able to attack you like they did. Sorry about that. My bad. But the ninja are right, everyone. Fun's over. Time to go back to your cells."

The inmates growled.

"Who's gonna make us?" said Kruncha.

The warden sighed. "Okay, guys, you know the routine. We can do this the easy way, or the hard way."

The inmates didn't budge.

The warden sighed. He reached for his cell keys so he could release the ninja — but they were missing. "Gosh darn it," he said. "Forgot my keys again." He spoke into a walkie-talkie. "Guards, we're gonna need backup here. Code 567. All inmates out of cells. Better bring everyone."

There was an awkward silence as the warden's walkie-talkie buzzed with static.

"Uh, guards?" the warden repeated.

Still static.

The inmates chuckled ominously.

"Well, well," rasped the Mechanic. "Did your backup take a lunch break?"

The warden looked to Dareth. "Did you see the guards outside on your way in?"

"The . . . guards? Outside?" Dareth stammered. "Ohhhhhhhhh. Is that who those people were? I thought they were backup camera crew."

The warden blinked. "No. Those were the prison guards. Who keep the dangerous inmates in check. With handcuffs. And stun guns. And balls and chains."

"Ah, uh . . ." Dareth scratched the back of his head. "I may have sent them for lunch. For all of us. And the editing team."

"You WHAT!?" cried the ninja and the warden.

"Hey, don't blame me!" cried Dareth. "Ninja gotta eat, baby. I thought after you guys talked the secret out of the inmates, we'd all enjoy a nice chat-and-chew ourselves. You know, take five."

Jay smacked his head. "This is bad, guys. *Really* bad."

Zane nodded. "I'm afraid it is indeed. Without our powers . . ."

"And locked up in this vengestone cell . . ." added Cole.

The Mechanic sneered as he took hold of Dareth and Warden Noble by their collars. "Looks like it's just you and us."

Chapter 9

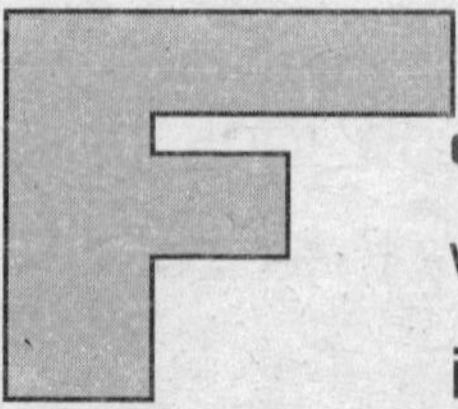

For the first time, Dareth was starting to get a bad feeling about this.

"Hey, come on, guys. I'm sure we can talk this out."

The Mechanic gave Dareth a rough shove into several other inmates. They pinned his arms.

"Like I said," the Mechanic said, sneering, "I got a bone to pick with the ninja. And since you seem pretty important to them, I think I'll start with you."

"He's not that important to us," Cole mumbled under his breath.

Kai elbowed him. "Guys, what are we going to do?"

"We can't do anything unless we get out of this cell," whispered Lloyd. "And the only way out is with the Mechanic's remote."

"Which I could zap out of his hands if I had my powers." Jay moaned.

"Too bad the only power Dareth has is the power of hot air," muttered Cole.

A funny look crossed Lloyd's face. "Guys . . . that might just be it!" He turned to the Mechanic. "You'd better not hurt him! Because if you mess with one ninja, you mess with all of us!"

The inmates laughed.

"He looks funny, yes," said Soto. "But a pajama man he be not."

"That's what you think," said Jay. "Really,

he's the strongest ninja of them all. He's the BROWN Ninja."

Dareth felt a bead of sweat run down his forehead.

"Guys," he said. "Normally I'd welcome the praise, but now's not the time."

"Seriously, he's more powerful than all of us," called Lloyd. "I just hope you make it out in one piece."

Nuckal eyed Dareth suspiciously. "If he's a ninja, then how come I saw him on the rec-room television the other day saying he was a — a manager. Or something."

"That was not me," said Dareth.

Nuckal shook his head. "I'm sure it was you. On *Fred Finley Live at Five*."

"You are mistaken," said Dareth.

"Enough of this!" cried the Mechanic. "If you're a ninja, *ninja*, then show us what you can do. Boys, lock up the warden. I don't want anyone interrupting."

The inmates pushed the warden into a cell and slammed the door shut. The Mechanic used the remote to lock it.

Dareth caught a glimpse of the remote just as the inmates shoved him into the center of their group. They jeered, forming a tight circle around him.

"Uh, guys." Dareth glanced pleadingly at the ninja. "I could really use some of that Master Wu mumbo jumbo right about now."

"Don't worry, Dareth," said Lloyd. "Just show him that power you're always *bragging* about."

"But I don't —" sputtered Dareth.

"Trust us!" cried Lloyd.

Dareth gulped as the Mechanic came right up in his face.

"So," the Mechanic said, "who wants a piece of the Brown Ninja first?"

"Me, me!" cried the inmates.

"You!" The Mechanic pointed to a Stone Warrior. "Teach him a lesson."

Dareth backed up as the Stone Warrior approached him.

"Uh," gulped Dareth. "Don't come too close! I don't want to hurt you."

The Stone Warrior didn't laugh. It didn't even blink. It just came closer.

"Don't say I didn't warn you!" exclaimed Dareth. "Here, I'll even tell you what I'm going to do. I'm going to, uh, beat you with that boulder over there. Yes!" He pointed to a boulder left on the ground from Cole's battle against Soto's crew. "I'm going to use my awesome ninja power to beat you with that boulder. Don't believe me? Just try to pick it up and see if you can throw it higher than I could. Go on. Try."

Now the Stone Warrior was confused. It looked at the boulder, and then at Dareth. With a shrug, it picked up the boulder easily. Then it tossed it up into the air and let it fall back to the ground.

"Hah! That was nothing," said Dareth. "My

grandmother could throw it higher. Try again. I want a real challenge to compete against."

The Stone Warrior frowned. It picked up the boulder and tossed it higher into the air. It landed with a *thud*.

"Better." Dareth nodded. "But the Brown Ninja is not impressed. Give me a true challenge, or let me face off against another opponent."

Now the Stone Warrior was angry. With a mighty heft, it lifted the boulder high into the air and chucked it up toward the ceiling.

CRASH!

The boulder landed right back on top of the Stone Warrior, knocking him out cold!

The inmates all gasped.

"See!" cried Lloyd. "Told you — the Brown Ninja defeats all!"

"Better throw your best fighter at him. Because no one is stronger than him!" shouted Cole.

"Cole!" the other ninja hissed.

"Oops," muttered Cole. "Well, he kind of deserves it, don't you think?"

"All right," the Mechanic said. "How about you?" He pointed to Soto. "Give him a taste of steel."

Soto snickered as he stepped forward. He leaned down and pulled the long, sharp fork he'd been using as a peg leg out from under him. Another inmate handed him a broomstick to use for a leg instead.

"So, pajama man," said Soto. "This may not be me sword, but I'd wager it can still make a mark or two."

"That's, uh, a cool accent you got there," said Dareth. "Too bad it's not how a real pirate sounds."

"A real —" Captain Soto sputtered. "What be ye talkin' about? I be the most fearsome pirate to ever captain a ship!"

"Sure, sure," said Dareth. "That sort of talk would pass on a movie set. But if you were really sailing the high seas, you'd need a saltier dialect than that."

Soto growled. "Be ye saying that I, Soto, the only pirate brave enough to steer a galleon upstream against the northern gall with a leaky hull, not be a true pirate in me words?"

"Mmmm-hmmm, mmmm-hmmm," said Dareth. "I'm starting to hear it. Loosen your jaw a little to make it more natural."

Now Captain Soto was enraged.

"How dare ye?" he snarled. "There ain't no other pirate as swashbucklin' as meself! Why I've led me crew to the very depths of the underworld and back in search of treasure you *pajama men* have only read about in your granddaddy's storybooks!"

With a mighty thrust, Captain Soto slammed his fork sword into the floor for emphasis.

Thud! The fork got stuck!

Soto frowned and pulled at the fork. But it

was good and stuck. Soto pulled harder and harder, until . . .

THWANG!

The fork sword sprang loose all at once, and Soto crashed back into his pirate crew. They toppled over and tumbled into a nearby cell.

Dareth couldn't help himself. He slicked back his hair.

"Who's next?"

"Enough!" hollered the Mechanic. He stomped right up in Dareth's face. "It's time to settle this once and for all."

Chapter 10

"Are you sure you want to face off against the Legendary Brown Ninja?" asked Dareth. He was starting to get the hang of this. "Let me know now if I should go easy on you."

The Mechanic grabbed Dareth by the throat with his robotic arm.

"Dareth!" cried the ninja.

"Ulp!" Dareth choked. "It's okay, guyzzz — I got dizz!"

"So," rasped the Mechanic. "Should I try flinging you around like that boulder? Or dis-assembling you limb from limb?"

Dareth mustered all his energy to keep from blacking out. "That's a strong grip you got there," he gasped. "Are you sure you want to take me on?"

"As sure as I want to crush every bone in your body," said the Mechanic.

"You're sure, sure?" asked Dareth. He grasped the Mechanic's robotic arm with both hands. "Or you think you're sure?"

"I *know* I'm sure," growled the Mechanic.

"Then think fast!" gasped Dareth.

With one quick motion, Dareth pressed the big red release button on the remote control in the Mechanic's hand.

The ninja's cell door sprang open!

"NINJA-GO!!!"

In a swirl of red, blue, green, black, and white Spinjitzu, the ninja whirled out of the vengestone cell and caught up all the prisoners in one gigantic tornado. For an instant, the only thing the warden and Dareth could see was a whirl-wind of dust, smoke, and flailing arms and legs.

When the ninja were through, all the prisoners sat tied up in bits of their own prison uniforms, lumped together in one giant pile. Last but not least was the Mechanic. Jay rocket-punched him to the very top of the pile.

Dareth dropped to the floor, gasping.

"You okay?" Kai asked Dareth.

Dareth gasped. "Never better."

Lloyd clapped him on the back. "Told you," he called to the inmates. "No one messes with the Brown Ninja."

Just then, the guards returned, carrying dozens of takeout bags.

"Did we miss something?" the head guard asked.

Later that evening, the six ninja and Dareth sat at Master Chen's Noodle House. Dareth had called ahead and asked Skylor for a favor. This evening, the ninja would enjoy the restaurant all to themselves. No media. No fans. Just friends.

"Come to papa," said Cole as he dumped a bowl full of puffy potstickers into his mouth. "Oh my gawd, guys." He munched. "It tastes so good when it hits your lips."

"Thanks for getting us the place all to ourselves, Dareth," said Nya. "After this, I'd say you only have 99,999 favors left to go before you don't owe us anymore."

Dareth waved away the remark with his chopsticks. "Don't be silly. I knew what I was doing all along."

"Really?" Jay cocked an eyebrow. "You knew you were sending us into a minefield of dangerous criminals with a vengestone cell in their arsenal?"

"So I was fuzzy on a few details," said Dareth. "But hey, you guys got to show off your teamwork or whatever that you're always talking about. So, you're welcome."

"Well, I hope you realize that we really are

done with all the celebrity stunts," said Lloyd. "No more interviews. No more setups. We can't always come to your rescue."

"Relax," said Dareth. "I've got my sights set on bigger goals now."

The ninja looked at one another.

"Really?" said Nya. "There's something bigger than interviews and press tours?"

"Yeah," said Kai. "Like what?"

Dareth smiled and took a big chomp out of a dumpling. "I realized today there's a true hero Ninjago City needs to know about. A hero who has been masked, hidden in the shadows, but no more."

"And that would be . . . ?" Cole asked.

"Me, of course!" exclaimed Dareth. "The Brown Ninja does indeed have real power! All this time, I've been the groupie to your boy band (plus one girl). Now I'm taking off on my own solo career. Yep, I've already planned out the promo: *Shrouded in Mystery: Who Is the Brown Ninja?* There will be book tours. Photo shoots. And an AUTHORIZED documentary. I'll be celebrity and manager all in one."

The ninja all groaned.

"Well, guys, he's finally done it," said Nya.

"Done what?" asked Jay.

"Tapped into his true potential," Nya said. "I don't think his head could get any bigger without exploding."

The ninja laughed as Dareth slurped down an entire bowl of noodles in one big gulp. "Gotta keep up my energy," he said.

Suddenly, Dareth's face turned bright red, and beads of sweat poured down from his hairline. "T-t-too . . . h-hot . . ." he stuttered, fanning his mouth. "T-t-oo . . . many . . . noodles . . . too much . . . h-heat . . ."

Lloyd laughed and handed Dareth a glass of water. "Like I told you guys," he said. "No one is stronger than the Brown Ninja when it comes to power — the power of hot air!"